Clifford's
Manners

Dedicated to Robbie and Alex

Copyright © 1987 by Norman Bridwell.

All rights reserved. Published by Scholastic Inc.
SCHOLASTIC, CARTWHEEL BOOKS, and associated logos are trademarks and/or registered
trademarks of Scholastic Inc.
CLIFFORD, CLIFFORD THE BIG RED DOG, BE BIG, and associated logos are registered trademarks of Norman Bridwell.

Library of Congress Cataloging-in-Publication Data

ISBN 978-0-545-21586-2

76   19 20

Printed in the U.S.A. 40
This edition first printing, September 2010

Clifford's
Manners

Norman Bridwell

SCHOLASTIC INC.

New York   Toronto   London   Auckland
Sydney   Mexico City   New Delhi   Hong Kong

I'm Emily Elizabeth,
and this is Clifford.

Everyone loves Clifford
because he has good manners.
I taught him myself.

Clifford says "please" when he asks for something.

Say please.

Say thank
you.

He says "thank you" when he gets something.

And he writes a thank-you note
when someone gives him a present.

Send
thank-you
notes.

Wait your turn.

Clifford loves to go to the movies.
He waits his turn in line.

If Clifford has a snack,
he puts the empty bag into the litter basket.
Clifford hates litterbugs.

Don't litter.

Say excuse
me.

Clifford says "excuse me" when he needs
to pass in front of people.

He never talks during the show.
Talking disturbs others.

**Do not talk
during a show.**

Use your handkerchief.

KERTY-SHOO!

When Clifford has to sneeze,
he uses a handkerchief or tissue.
It's a good thing he does.

Clifford has many friends.
He shares his toys with them.

Share.

Put your
toys away.

Clifford puts his toys away when he is through.
His friends help. They have good manners, too.

Clifford is a terrific tennis player.
He obeys all the rules of the game.

Follow the rules.

Talk—
don't hit.

Sometimes players disagree.
When Clifford is angry, he does not hit.
He just says what he feels.

Clifford is a good sport.
He smiles when he loses.
And he does not boast when he wins.

| CLIFFORD | 4 | 4 | 5 |
| EMILY | 6 | 6 | 7 |

Be a good
sport.

Call ahead.

Clifford loves to go visiting.
When he visits his sister in the country,
he always calls ahead.

Clifford always arrives on time.

Don't be late.

Knock before
you walk in.

He knocks on the door before he enters.

He wipes his feet first.

Wipe your feet.

Shake hands.

Clifford kisses his sister.
He shakes hands with her friend.

Wash up
before
you eat.

Clifford's sister has dinner ready.
Clifford washes his hands before he eats.

Clifford chews his food with his mouth closed.
He never talks with his mouth full.

**Don't talk
with your
mouth full.**

Help
clean up.

Clifford helps with the cleanup.

Say
good-bye.

Then he says "thank you" and "good-bye"
to his sister and to his friend.

Everyone loves Clifford's manners.
That's why everyone loves Clifford!

Have good
manners.